The Little Knight

Written by Nettie Stather   Illustrated by Suzie Dennis

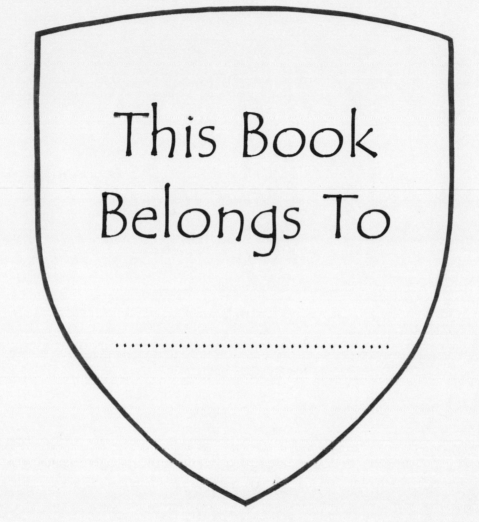

This Book
Belongs To

....

Down the lane and over the ford,

the little knight stood with his trusty sword.

He yearned for adventure, to be gallant and bold.

To rescue fair maidens and find treasures of gold.

He jumped on his horse and rode through the fields,

his sword in his belt and a shiny gold shield.

'Wait' cried a voice as the brave knight looked back.

It was George the Jester with a dirty old sack.

'Can I come with you in search of a quest?'

The knight felt quite lonely so the two headed west.

Around the big mountains and
through the tall trees,
they stumbled across a
chest full of keys.

George took the keys and started to joke,

'Let's look for some treasure, I'll dig by this oak.'

Out of the sack came a rusty brown shovel.

They dug a huge hole but they only found rubble.

'A ha' cried a voice near the patch where they sat,

as a wizard appeared with a black pointy hat.

'Can I come with you in search of a beast?'

and with that the friends journeyed on to the east.

Ahead lay a river,

which they crossed in a boat.

In the distance was a castle with a

drawbridge and moat.

At the top of the castle in a scary cold tower,

a beautiful damsel stood holding a flower.

As she picked at the petals she longed to be freed,

wishing for her hero to do a great deed.

'Stop!' hissed a dragon who came out of the dark.

She breathed fire from her nostrils which lit up with a spark!

'If you come any closer you'll end up in my mouth!

So I suggest you about turn and start heading south.'

N
W E
S

'I've an idea' said the handsome old wizard.

He raised up his wand and changed

dragon to lizard.

To the highest most step climbed the victorious three.

The top door was locked, they must find the key!

George tried the keys from the chest they had found.

The door finally opened with a loud creaking sound.

'Hooray!'

cried the maiden finally freed from her jail.

'I knew there would be a happy ending to this tale.'

'Your reward is a wish for the dragon that you fought,'

but adventure and friendship was all that they sought.

'Brave Knight, Handsome Wizard,
Jester George, Little Lizard.'

'Your quest must continue, to lands far and new.

I search for my prince now,

so can I come too?'

but which way would they go forth?...

...of course they went north!

First published in Great Britain in 2009
Nettie Stather
www.thelittleknight.com
info@thelittleknight.com

The moral right of the author has been asserted
A CIP catalogue record of this book is available from the
British Library

ISBN 978 0 9554433 0 5

Printed in Hong Kong by Regal Printing Limited
Typeset by Nettie Stather